getting CORPORATE

AF757033

getting CORPORATE

Clare Maxfield

wisdom tree

Published in 2006 by

wisdom tree

wisdom tree
4779/23, Ansari Road, Darya Ganj, New Delhi-110002
Ph.: 23247966/67/68

First published by Ibis Publishing Australia

Copyright © Clare Maxfield 2005

ISBN 81-8328-055-2

All rights reserved. No part of this publication may be reproduced, stored in a retrieval system or transmitted in any form or by any means, electronic, mechanical, photocopying, recording or otherwise, without the prior written permission of the copyright owner. Enquiries should be made to the publisher.

Cover and text designed by Kinart
Cover illustration by Wai

Printed at Print Perfect, New Delhi-110064

contents

introduction

Do you have what it takes to make your mark in the corporate market? Grades will help you get a great job, as will the right clothes and the perhaps the right connections, but do you have what it takes to make it to the top and stay there? There is a percentage of people out there who happily make it through life existing and just getting the job done, and then there are those who seem to move up the ranks with supersonic speed.

Knowing how to look is half the challenge; the other half is how to act so that you not only fit in, but you stand out for all of the right reasons. Understanding the daily challenges of office politics, or the office games as I prefer to call them, will keep you out of trouble. Knowing how to manage your way through business meetings and what to do to stand out from the crowd is an effective way of ensuring that management come to know, respect, trust and—most of all—like you.

'Proper preparation prevents poor performance' is a quote by American quarterback Charlie Batch. It is well known that the better prepared you are the better your chances to succeed. This is a given for anything that you do in life. Leaving anything to chance is leaving a door open for failure to creep in.

Unexpected office situations can be trying enough, but what do you do when you are invited to dine with a client in a manner to which you are not yet accustomed? How do you handle the tricky etiquette of the corporate golf day? Or the confusion of dealing with strangers from other countries?

Your future is in your hands and you are the sole creator of how well and how far you can go in this life. Don't allow mediocrity to be your lot. You have the ability to do whatever you want.

I hope through reading *Getting Corporate* that a wealth of doors will open to you and your future possibilities will be endless. Take the chance to make your mark on the corporate world starting here.

Clare Maxfield
www.claremaxfied.com.au

acknowledgements

Getting Corporate came together with the help and support of so many people and I would like to take this opportunity to let everyone know how much I truly appreciate them.

Closest to home I must thank Mum for her unfailing support and my brother Colin who was my advisor on the corporate golf tips. As the manager of two golf courses, who better to go to? It was an interesting way to spend our afternoon on Christmas day. Warren Dennison for his insights into NZ culture as well as Lisa Miller and Simon Clarke who helped me with most of Asia.

From Ibis I have to thank Margaret, Pam and Anthony for all of their hard work and belief in my series. Thanks again to Sally for her editing skills in making sense out of what I write. To my agent Brett Osmond, you started this amazing adventure for me and I thank you every time I see one of my books in a store. Also to Jane for your fabulous typing skills: you managed to get both my written word and poor dictation into legible script in a very quick time.

Others who had a hand in inspiring portions of what I have written are Anne Tustin, Suzanne and Rohan, my NSAA colleagues—especially Helen Macdonald— my clients through Corporate Confidence and all my friends who gave me the encouragement and ideas to complete this book.

Lastly, as always, my thanks go to my wonderful husband Ngoc. You are the best thing that ever happened to me. You give me time, you give me love and you give me friendship. What more can a girl ask for in life?

I am blessed to have great family, great friends and a great life. Believe me: if you focus on great things happening, they do.

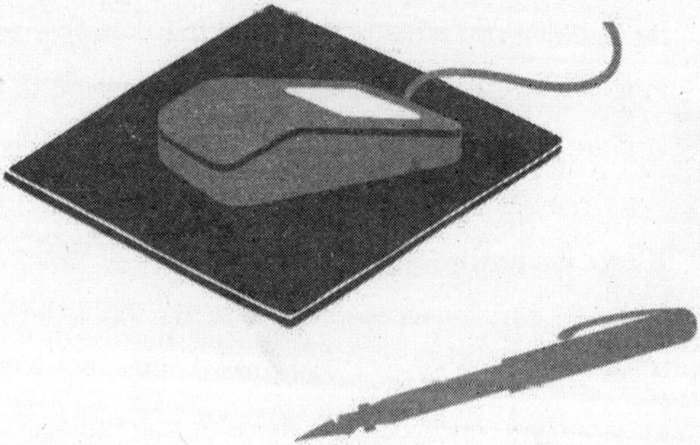

etiquette

✱ Show you care

Maintaining eye contact for 80% of a conversation will show that you are interested and that you are listening to a person.

✱ Don't look away

Be careful if you are a person who thinks deeply and has to look away. Ensure the person you are speaking to knows you are thinking about their issue, and not another subject.

✱ Keep it clean

It can be easy for some people to slip a four-letter word into a conversation in the heat of the moment. This will only cheapen you and your argument. A true professional has a broad enough vocabulary to find words that are cleaner and far more cutting.

✱ Take your turn

It is great to be brimming with ideas or passionate about a subject but there is no value to be gained by jumping in and talking over everyone. Wait your turn. People will listen when you have something to say if you wait for the correct moment to say it.

✱ Be thoughtful in your questions

Asking a lot of questions is nowhere near as effective as asking a few well-thought-out questions. My bookkeeper Anne told me how she has climbed her corporate ladder by asking a few well-chosen questions of the right people. It was the quality of her questions that put her ahead of others in her field.

* Don't fidget

Fidgets may as well be saying, 'Get me out of here'. Pen clickers, paper rustlers, leg jigglers—they are all the same. If you have a tendency to any or all of the above, get some stillness in your life and focus on not moving around so much. It can be very distracting to others.

* Don't roll your eyes

Have you noticed that when there is a group discussion on a reality show, someone will be shown to be rolling their eyes at a comment made? You will get ahead further by keeping such responses to yourself. In management you sometimes have to work with people you may not choose to socialise with, but the company will hire the best people for the job and you all need to work together.

*** Keep your arms by your side unless you are cold**

Body language 101—crossing your arms creates a barrier between you and the person you are talking to. Open up communication by keeping your body open to others.

*** Women: beware of using the sexy neck routine**

We women are often not aware of how we use our bodies to motivate a response from a person. Tilting your head back to expose your neck makes you appear more vulnerable. It may work with boyfriends but don't use it in business; you won't be taken seriously.

*** Touching can be tricky**

Don't get caught out trying to get someone's attention and being accused of harassment. The safest place to touch someone is on the arm between the elbow and the shoulder. Don't leave your actions open for misinterpretation.

*** Become a mirror**

If you are having difficulty getting through to a person, mirror their actions. Unconsciously they will start relating to you more.

*** Keep your face open**

Unless you are about to sneeze or cough you should never cover your mouth or face. Any barrier to your face for the person you are speaking to can be perceived as a disguise for a lie. Even placing a finger to your mouth or nose could be taken as hiding something.

electronic etiquette

Whilst the computer age was hailed as a means of making life easier, it has resulted in taking up more of our time both at work and at home. It has also opened up a whole new range of etiquette issues to be dealt with daily.

Email

* **Always use the subject line**

Due to the huge amount of mail received by many people daily, the subject line is often the decider used on whether to open a letter or not. It also helps to sort emails into their folders. I tend to treat an email as suspicious if it has no subject and will often delete it.

* **Break the chain**

What more can I say? Living in a time where we should fill our thoughts with positive affirmations, the last thing I need is to be threatened with a lack of good fortune because I did not forward some sappy chain email to other people less interested than I in the next nanosecond.

* **Use the 'bcc' function**

You can land yourself in a lot of hot water by exposing other people's email addresses. When sending out an email to a group of people, send the mass of addresses from the blind carbon copy ('bcc') line and one to yourself in the 'To' line. It will save any embarrassment.

*** Create a signature for your emails**

Often I will pick up the phone to respond to an email if it is starting to get tricky. It can become a hassle if I then have to look up the contact details. At the bottom of each email you should have your name, company, phone numbers and email details. It is also an excellent place to promote your business either through a by-line or a link to your website.

*** Never assume the worst**

If you do not hear from someone in reply to an email, never assume they are simply not responding. In the past six months I have had a dreaded intermittent bug that has attacked some emails but not others. In this instance I was not receiving emails and people sending them were never aware of the problem. If it is important, follow it up with a call.

* **Avoid SMS spam**

  Whenever you send an SMS text message to someone, ensure you include your details. It's a matter of courtesy, and it's practical, too.

* **Mind your spam**

  We have rules now to protect us from spam mail. To save yourself from breaching any laws, it is safest to invite people to receive your company newsletter. You can do this by asking directly or by sending out a copy to people you have met and asking them to let you know if they would like to subscribe.

* **Write like an adult, not a phone message**

  SMS is the modern shorthand. It is very disconcerting to receive emails written in SMS text. You may be sending it from a phone but others might not be receiving it that way. It's a faux pas in a world where image matters.

✱ Check your spelling

Use spell check on every letter you send out. It takes only a second and will always make you look educated. It helps to have your system set to automatically spell check every email you send.

✱ Write what you would say

Only send in an email what you would say to someone's face. Remember, it is not like a letter that you can rip up. If you hit 'send' before 'delete' there is no going back.

✱ Don't yell

Just because you are no longer in your Grade 5 English class, there is no reason to forget your grammar. Emails written entirely using upper case is the same as yelling at a person.

* Respect everyone's space

It is fine to send a straight reply to a person but if this banter goes on you should delete unnecessary text on the subsequent emails. Use and retain only what is relevant to that response or event. Completely delete all historical notes as you should have them on file in the earlier emails.

Mobile manners

* Keep It discreet

You may like loud music, science fiction movies or animal noises but no one else needs to be distracted by said noises coming from your phone. Keep the ring tone discreet enough so it won't take your colleagues' minds from their job.

✱ There is no need to yell

In a public place don't speak so loudly that everyone in the next room can hear your conversation. If the line is faint, go to where you can speak more loudly without disturbing everyone.

✱ Keep it handy

If you are going to carry your phone with you in public places, keep it in an accessible place. So many women have them in the bottom of their handbag and don't find them until it is too late to retrieve the call.

✱ Know when to turn it off

Leaving your phone on during a meeting is telling the person you are dealing with that there is something more important than they are. Show respect for the person you are meeting with by turning your phone off.

✱ It is not a piece of cutlery

Therefore it should not sit on the table. Unless there is an extenuating circumstance—and waiting for a date to call is not one—there is no need to leave your phone visible on a table.

✱ How to handle the extenuating circumstance

If you have to leave the phone on, always advise the people you are meeting that there is a call you are waiting on and that you must take it. In this instance it would be wise to put your phone on silent and vibrate. Ensure when the call comes through that you walk away to take it and then turn your phone off when you are finished.

*** Keep your focus on the meeting**

A habit seems to be forming of using meetings to send SMS and now emails from blackberries. This is rude and very unprofessional. No matter what sort of high flyer you are, you should never treat any meeting or any person with such lack of professional courtesy.

*** Calls can wait**

If you are making calls from home and have 'call waiting', let the incoming call go if you are on a business call.

office politics

* It's not politics: it's a game

I'm not a great one for understanding how politics works but I do know the basic rules of game playing. Learn the rules so you know how the game is played. Understand the rules and you will also understand the consequences of breaking them.

Breaking a rule because you choose to is in your control, but breaking a rule you were not aware existed is ignorance. Ignorant people do not get far in life. Choose to go as far as you can by learning how the rules will work for you. Know the rules, know the competition and know where the game finishes—your goal—and just keep playing until you get there.

* Getting along at work—what really happens?

Do your work, keep your mouth shut and you will get ahead. Right? Wrong! Yes, it is important to do your work but make sure it is known as your work before someone else takes the credit.

*** Go the extra yard**

No one is indispensable today, but by making yourself useful you can save your skin when cutbacks occur. This doesn't mean doing someone else's job, as they can take the credit. Instead, find ways to save the company time and money and where possible assign yourself to them. When management sees how you can help the company you will become an asset to them.

*** Don't be a 'yes' person**

Jumping at the chance to do everything and agreeing to everything you hear does not necessarily make you important, but it can give you overload. Agree to do the work you know you can do well rather than putting your hand up for anything, or you will end up finishing nothing.

✱ Party on, dude

Get known socially as well as professionally. You don't need to stay out all night and be the life of the party but many a position has arisen from who you know rather than what you know. If you get to know someone socially they are more likely to help you when the need arises.

✱ It takes one to know one

Socialising with others in your office makes them more aware of who you are and it might just be your name that comes to mind for a promotion or special project.

✱ Be an ambassador, not a politician

Ambassadors represent their country or product and are well respected and trusted with the integrity of the product. Politicians can be seen as hand shakers, who smile too much and don't deliver the truth. Place yourself as one who can be trusted and relied upon to do the best for your company or department.

✱ Play fair

In the corporate world you can either play fair and concede a few losses or play dirty and step on everyone to win. The first option will get you further in the long run. I'm not advocating being a rug for everyone to wipe their feet on—that won't work—but certainly holding a few doors for others will get repaid in the long run.

✱ Gender tender—all is fair in love and war

Today women are getting as far in business as men and the future will find an even greater balance of the sexes at the top. A message to all men: listen to both your male and female colleagues. Sexist comments and attitudes are noticed, and will not further your career.

showing respect

* **Open the doors for those behind you**

  When you approach a door as a group it is polite for the first person to open the door and hold it for the entire group. If you don't know the people behind you, and it is a large group not attached to you, hold the door for the next person and they will do the same for the person following them and so on. If you are walking with someone superior or elderly it is polite to hold the door open for them.

* **Last in, first out of the elevator**

  Elevators don't have a lot of room for niceties, so if you are closest to the door you should exit first.

*** If someone is in trouble give them a hand**

There is nothing wrong with helping someone who is having trouble getting their coat on, struggling with parcels or opening the car door. As long as it is a natural situation and you are doing it because there is a genuine need, as opposed to making yourself appear better for it.

*** Always be on time**

Your bosses may not notice how early you get to work but they definitely notice if you are late. Don't feel that an extra five minutes here or ten minutes there won't matter. If you are going to be late, let someone know and stay behind to make up the time. Don't make a habit of it though, or your superiors will find someone else to take your position.

✱ Don't get involved in the soap operas

There is always someone who knows everything about everyone in the office. As tempting as it might be to stand in the tea room and listen to the gossip, be assured that if you are listening to gossip about other people, when you're not around they will be gossiping about you. It is safest to just remove yourself from the situation and not get involved.

✱ If you are not comfortable—say so

Sometimes people get so comfortable with colleagues that they can forget themselves and say or do things which they would usually reserve for their friends. It can be a compliment that you have made someone feel comfortable enough around you for them to do that, but clearly let them know if you are uncomfortable. With a smile, tell those people that they're stepping over the line. If you do it nicely they won't be offended and the conversation should easily continue.

* Nothing personal—its just business

The greatest mistake you can make in business is to take everything too personally. If you are doing the job you are employed to do and you get resistance or abuse from someone, remember it is not you they are attacking. Develop a thicker skin to shrug off such incidents.

* Get off my turf

Don't let someone come in and take over your decision-making process or your presentation. This is a play used by pushy people to make their presence felt and their ideas heard.

* He said, she said

Don't allow yourself to get caught up in company politics of 'he said, she said'. You will be playing their game, not yours. Repeat only what you know and what is relevant to the business at hand.

* Don't spit the dummy

The adult versions of dummy spitting, foot stomping and childish tantrums are threats and backstabbing. Be warned: word of these actions does reach the top and will not leave you looking professional or mature.

managing meetings

* **Keep it snappy**

  An ill-prepared meeting is unprofessional. Know the most important objectives: what you are going to discuss, with whom, what your desired outcome is and its timeline.

* **Plan it**

  Write out a detailed outline of what the meeting is about and the objectives.

* **Invite the attendees**

  Now that you know what you want to achieve in this meeting you will know who you should invite.

* **Select your location**

  While coffee shops seem ideal for informal meetings, keep in mind the space and the noise.

Etiquette tip: if you have invited a person you do not know well out for a coffee chat/meeting be prepared to pay for their drink as you instigated the invitation. On further meetings this is not necessary.

* Put it in writing

The agenda of the meeting needs to be sent to everyone involved in advance. This allows the attendees, you included, to ensure they have everything they require for the meeting.

* Straight talkers need 75% of the time

If your meeting is mainly for informing your group of something, allow a quarter of the time for questions and the bulk of the time for delivering the information.

*** Discussions deserve time**

Be sure not to underestimate the time required for a group discussion. In this instance allow 50% of the time for the presentation and 50% for a discussion of the topic at hand.

*** Stick to the time allowed**

It is frustrating and unprofessional for a meeting to take longer than the allocated time. If a discussion is going to take longer, allocate another time to meet. Not everyone's schedule may be as flexible as yours.

*** Listen to what is being said**

Never assume you know what a person wants or is asking for. In any meeting, ensure you take notes on what was said; listen, and note key words and phrases.

✱ Look at the speaker

Body language can give us so many more clues than words so make sure you are looking at the speaker. Their body language will show you what is most important to them.

✱ Don't draw your own conclusions

This is especially relevant if you are asked to do something which seems foreign or is difficult to understand. You need to understand exactly what is being asked, so ask questions to help you understand the reasoning.

✱ Don't butt in

Check first if the speaker will allow you to ask questions during the presentation. Never butt in over what someone else is trying to say.

* **Make notes of questions**

  Once a question is formed in our minds we might not hear anything else that is being said. Write down your questions as they come to mind so you free yourself to listen. Ask your questions at a more relevant time. If you have a lot of questions, you may wish to ask them privately after the session.

networking

* **Rank rules supreme**

When trying to decide who should be introduced to whom, remember that the most important person gets introduced to the other person. If both people are of equal rank, introduce the woman to the man to show courtesy, or simply introduce the first arrival or the person nearest to you. In large groups, people of equal ranking often introduce themselves to each other.

* **Add some background**

If you are hosting an event, include a little background information on each person when you introduce them, especially if they have something in common. This will open up a conversation between those two and leave you free to talk to others.

*** It's fine to ask about pronunciation**

Many names today are not as simple as Mary, Paul or David. If you have been introduced to someone whose name sounds foreign to you or you missed the pronunciation, it is fine to ask to hear the name again. This is better than mistakenly calling someone by the wrong name, or using the wrong pronunciation.

*** Never assume familiarity**

Only use first names when you are invited to do so. If you are given a surname only, use it until invited to do otherwise.

*** Cards are a must**

Always arrive at a network event with your business cards. If you are out of cards, run some basic cards through your printer before you leave for any event.

* **It doesn't have to be fancy**

Business cards are an important part of business. At the very least, make sure you include on your card your name and a contact number. In the corporate market, you should also include your email address, a postal address and your business name.

* **Keep your cards handy**

There is no point in going to a network event in the hope of getting to know others and having your cards tucked away so safely it takes forever to get to them. The inside pocket of your jacket is ideal. For women, if you don't have an inside pocket it is worth having one put into your jacket.

* **Separate your cards**

When you receive another person's card it is safest to put it in another pocket or space away from your own cards. It is very embarrassing to go to hand out one of your own cards only to give another person's, especially if they are competition to the person you are talking to.

*** Keep it neat**

No one wants to receive a nasty, dog-eared card. Your cards are a reflection of you, so keep them neat and clean.

*** Don't waste space**

You have two sides to your card. The front should have all of your relevant details; the back can be used as well. If you are dealing with international clients who speak another language, put all of your details in their language on the back. Alternatively, if your clients are local, use the back to give an idea about some of the work you do.

*** Be selective**

By this I don't mean you to be stingy with your cards, but don't hand them over just because you can. By all means strike up as many conversations as you can and exchange cards when it seems appropriate, but wait till you have at least had a conversation with someone and seen if there is any purpose in exchanging your cards.

* **Use it or lose it**

  Once again, it is not how many cards you have but what you do with them. Practise the act of follow-up and all will be worthwhile.

* **Make contact**

  Depending on how your business operates, it is always nice to send a quick note the following day to the people you met. As this is not done that regularly it will make you stand out from the crowd.

* **Networking opens doors**

  Networking is a 'love it' or 'hate it' exercise. Good networkers always do better than people who stay at home or in their offices. It is through networking that you get to form social connections with people you may otherwise never have met.

* Joining the party

The safest and easiest way to join a conversation at a social function is with a group of three to six people. Any smaller and they may be in an intimate conversation and any larger and you can be left on the edge.

* Talk about the arts

Very safe subjects to talk about are films, theatre and any other arts that may be on in your area. You can talk about local shows or festivals that may be happening. This will often lead on to the performances, the stars, maybe some awards or coming attractions.

* The good old favourites—football and golf

All sports and hobbies are a very safe topic and are enjoyed by most people. The state and town you are in will determine what football league you will be talking about. But then again, you may also wish to talk about whatever your hobbies are. This can lead on to some experiences the other person may have had.

* Conversation taboos

We all know that the subjects to avoid are sex, religion and politics. Save these topics for your friends at a heated dinner party with lots of red wine; don't open conversations about these topics with someone you barely know.

* Have a good opening line

Know that at many functions you will be asked about your job. Rather than just saying 'I'm in sales', 'I'm in marketing' or 'I'm an accountant', add a little more information. Think of it as a fifteen-second elevator speech. You have only got a few seconds to say what you do to get someone's interest so that they will ask more questions.

✱ Listen for your clues

When you are in a conversation, look someone in the eye and truly listen to what they are saying. It can give you clues to lead the conversation in many more directions and save embarrassing silences with the two of you looking around for something else to discuss.

✱ Books bridge the gap

When I was travelling, I always knew what the latest books were by what other passengers were reading. Nowadays I rely on the top ten lists or what takes my interest. I have found that books can be the source of a very lengthy and interesting topic of conversation between strangers.

* What else is there?

So you have talked about sport, you've talked about the theatre and you have talked about books. Other topics you might want to talk about are music, shows you have seen, travel or places you have been. You may even want to talk about architecture and cities and of course, business. Generally, if you are at a networking event, the idea is to get to know a little about what the other person does and what type of business they are in. That way you can see if there is any synchronicity with your own business and how you may be able to help each other.

getting ahead

* **Make sure it is accurate**

  You may have written a fantastic presentation, an excellent memo or an amazing letter but if it is full of spelling errors or mathematical inaccuracies, incorrect grammar or punctuation mistakes you will find that people pay more attention to what you have done wrong rather than what you have done right.

* **Get a good attitude**

  Your attitude is how people perceive you. As I said earlier, treat this as a game, enjoy all you do, have a positive, 'no worries' attitude with everything you do and you will be a delight to work with. People will seek you out to help them in their area.

* **Fix it**

  There is no point complaining about something; it is up to you to fix it. If you can't fix it then find the person who can.

* Meet your deadlines

No matter what is going on in your life personally and privately, it should never affect your work. If you have deadlines to meet, make sure you hit those deadlines. A person who promises and never delivers will not get ahead.

* Learn to articulate

Once again, no matter how good your skills are, if you cannot speak properly you will never be put in a position where you have contact with outside people. You need to articulate well and speak in a well modulated voice. Have you noticed how professional speakers slow their speaking and generally speak in a slightly deeper tone? This is easier for men, but many times has to be worked on by women. Women, lose your squeak. It is very annoying to hear a woman speaking in a high-pitched tone. With a little practice you can change any high-pitched voice to a deeper, more modulated voice that is pleasing on the ear.

*** Don't always expect to be thanked**

You are being paid to do your job; you are not doing your boss a favour. You will be thanked if you have done a great job but don't expect to be thanked for every little thing you do along the way.

*** Keep it clean**

This relates to two areas. If your work area is clear and clean, your mind will be less cluttered and it will be easier for your fellow workers to work around you. At the same time, keep your language clean. You may love throwing those four-letter words around the football field with your mates but throwing them around the office does not show you have any grasp of the English language. If you want to throw an insult at someone, be creative with the words you use, as opposed to using some of the more inane and offensive four-letter words that we have floating around.

✱ Limit your personal stuff

Work is not the time to be making personal calls, sending personal emails, making personal comments about other people or discussing your personal problems. Of course you can do all this during your lunch hour, or before or after work, but don't spend your boss's time and money sorting out your own issues.

✱ Smoking is hazardous to your career

Smoking is now considered a sign of weakness rather than sophistication. Never light up if you don't see an ashtray.

corporate style

* Take a good look at yourself

The most valuable asset in your house is a full-length mirror. There is no point in thinking you look great only to hear the sniggers in the street when something is wrong.

* Look the part

How you dress will be how you are perceived initially. When you are meeting new clients your presentation is vital to your success. It helps if you present yourself in a way that clients expect. In the corporate market, traditional business and smart casual are as casual as you can go.

* Denim is disastrous

Denim is the lowest denominator in dressing. At any social function, you want to stand out and look successful. I would advise purchasing casual trousers to wear to the more casual events and saving your jeans for going out with friends.

*** It is not a pick-up joint**

Going to work is your professional life and not a time to be wearing your night-club clothes to attract attention. Keep your decorum and keep your job.

*** Keep it covered**

Any form of cleavage (or 'visible cracks' as a friend put it) should be hidden during working hours. Cleavage relates to busts, bums and toes. Cover them up and it will be your good work that is on display.

*** Why not sandals?**

Lately, a woman in a store was surprised when I would only look at covered shoes for work. She pointed out that there were plenty of nice sandals that women were wearing to work. However, having open toes just makes you that bit more casual or sexy. A very smartly dressed corporate woman will always wear shoes with the toes covered.

* Getting tied up

A tie is a must for a businessman. I know clients in the warmer states often don't wear a tie every day but they always have one on hand for when they have to attend a meeting. If you see plenty of businessmen walking around without ties you can bet your bottom dollar they are not going into a meeting.

* Hosiery finishes the look

Wearing hosiery in summer is as welcome as a tie is to a man, but it is just as necessary. Hosiery completes a corporate outfit and presents you in a very professional manner. To go without is to sabotage your look.

* Keep it unfussed

Going to a meeting and carrying both a handbag and a briefcase can look cumbersome. If you travel to see clients, leave your handbag locked in the boot of your car and transfer the minimum that you need into your satchel or briefcase. Looking cluttered will destroy your professional image.

*** Don't give them a headache**

Perfumes and aftershaves can be very potent so don't be liberal in your application. Keep your scent subtle and you won't scare anyone away or give them a headache. Some of the unisex fragrances are the easiest to wear.

*** Watch out for driver's fatigue**

I'm not talking about a powernap on the side of the road but the damage you do to your shoes when driving. Many of us clean up the fronts of our shoes regularly but forget about the backs of the heels. Keep a shoe sponge in your desk or glove box to ensure your shoes always look smart and clean.

accessories

*** Finish off your look**

Complete the picture that you know what you are doing by using the right accessories. With a traditional business suit, choose gold and silver classic pieces. As your clothing gets more relaxed so can your accessories, but don't try to wear surfie bracelets with a tailored suit. You wouldn't wear a suit to the beach so why wear anything surf-related to the office? The same goes for your compendiums, wallets and bags.

*** Carry a good pen**

This would have to be one of my top five tips. A good pen says something about you. Whether you are signing contracts or taking notes, it always pays to use quality products.

*** Choose a leather compendium**

If you need to take notes (and who doesn't?), attend a meeting with a stylish compendium that holds a notepad, a good-looking pen, spare business cards, room for cards you are given and a sleeve in which to put any letters. Ideally it should zip up so you don't have any slip ups.

*** Get a good wallet**

When you are out for drinks with colleagues or taking a client out for coffee, you don't want to pull out your Velcro wallet from your suit pocket or briefcase. A smart leather wallet will show you have style.

*** Keep your wallet organised**

Your wallet does not need to become your quarterly tax file: don't overstuff it with receipts. At the end of each week, make a habit of putting your receipts into a file to be handled when your tax needs to be done. An overstuffed wallet can also ruin your back if it stays in your back pocket while you sit on it all day.

*** Keep your wallet safe**

If you overstuff your wallet, it will not fit comfortably in your jacket or trouser pocket. You don't want it to be an easy target for a pickpocket.

✱ A briefcase needs to be in keeping with your look

In the corporate world you should really carry a leather briefcase. A hard shell, like a Samsonite briefcase, is great for a photographer or a special agent. Messenger bags will give you a very modern preppy look which is great for the less traditional industries that do not include finance or legal practices, but is not recommended for real estate either. Vinyl is for the person going nowhere fast, and all other man-made waterproof fabrics are too relaxed to be taken seriously.

✱ Don't carry your life in your hands

Your briefcase needs to carry what you need for your meetings, not for the rest of your life. Don't fill it with your junk. Keep only what you need to get your job done. If you tend to overstuff it, make a habit of regularly cleaning it out.

first impressions

* Why bother?

Whether it is your first day on the job or you are meeting someone for the first time, you will be judged on how you come across. This first impression will decide how you are thought of in the future.

* It's so superficial

Yes, initial impressions can be very superficial so be aware of this. There is nothing wrong in making sure you look the part to play the part. Once this superficial assessment is over, your personality and more of what is inside will come into play. Until you have established yourself, you need to ensure you create the right impression with everyone you meet.

* Ten seconds to victory

Within the first few seconds of meeting someone, they will decide if they like you or not, whether they trust you and whether they care to spend any more time with you in or out of business. If this first impression is positive you are on the road to successful negotiations and interactions in the future.

* What are you worth?

I have a magnet given to me by a friend that states 'good clothes open all doors'. You want people to look at you and see success and value, not a struggling try-hard. Emulate the appearance of successful people in your industry.

* **Trust is evident**

  Your image will dictate whether or not people feel they can trust you. Your clients will want to trust that you can deliver on your promises. This is not a time to try new and exciting looks and have them question your integrity, your ability to do the job or your dedication to a project.

* **Looking important**

  You don't want someone preferring to do business with a subordinate because they look more important than you. To be successful you must dress as if you are successful already.

✱ Sophistication speaks for itself

Sophistication can be simple. It is a sign you have matured and are sure of yourself. To gain this level of respect the simplest method is to forgo the trappings of your youth. By this I mean the party ties and socks for men and, for women, the ponytails and girlish hair accessories. The corporate world is a sophisticated market that rewards its own.

✱ Look intelligent

Geniuses may be able to take their own road in the manner of dress they choose. People wanting to get ahead without the benefit of genius need to present themselves in an intelligent manner. That is by creating confidence in their ability by the manner of their dress.

* **What you see is what you get**

  Make sure your image is in keeping with what you do for a living. It will ease any confusion in the long run and open the doors to many discussions much more quickly.

* **Dress the part**

  'When in Rome do as the Romans do.' Find out what the dress code is for the situation you are entering and dress accordingly. There is no room for winging it here. Once you have the trust of those you are meeting with, your personality can shine through.

* **Your handshake is your key**

  One of your first contacts with a person is when you shake their hand. This first impression is lasting: make sure that any time you are meeting someone you extend your hand and shake it. Contact has been made and you have a great chance of the person remembering you in the future.)

* Shake hands with confidence

There is no excuse for a poor handshake. You should connect with the other person's hand at the webbing between their thumb and forefinger, close your fingers over their hand firmly and shake for two to three pumps of your hands.

* Shake it, don't break it

Some men like to shake hands with force to show their manliness. Keep in mind this forceful shake is not appropriate for women. A man in a presentation once grilled me on varying cultures and how, if you shook an Indian woman's hand, it should be very limp. Surprised, I asked him to demonstrate what he called limp. To me it was a comfortable handshake so I asked him to demonstrate a true handshake. I think I managed to get the blood flowing some minutes later. He had no idea how strong his handshake was to a woman.

* **Wet fish don't fly**

A wet fish or limp handshake can say a few different things. You either don't know how to shake hands, you are hesitant to shake hands, or you have no respect for the hand you are shaking. None of the above is acceptable; learn to shake properly.

* **Keep it local**

Understand the area you are in and the customs of the country. In Australia, handshakes are the norm in business introductions. Hugs and kisses are considered very European and can cause distress and confusion to someone who is not expecting it.

* **When to extend**

You should always extend your hand in greeting when you are meeting someone for the first time, meeting someone you haven't seen for a while, greeting your host(ess), greeting guests, saying good-bye to people at a gathering or if someone else extends a hand.

*** Handshaking tip**

If your hands tend to be clammy, spray them with antiperspirant at least once a day. Also avoid giving a cold, wet handshake by keeping your drink in the left hand.

*** People like the sound of their own name**

Earn yourself brownie points and even imprint a person's name on your memory by repeating it often. People feel special when you use their name.

*** Look them in the eye**

Once again, while someone is trying to determine what sort of person you are, they will be looking in your eyes. Maintain about 80% of your eye contact with a person by looking them square in the eye. You want to be seen as confident and self-assured and eye contact will do that for you. People who look away or appear shifty are not able to look someone in the eye.

*** Smile and the world smiles with you**

No matter how nervous you are, how uncomfortable you are, how much you are sweating over the types of questions they are going to ask you, as long as you are smiling it gives you a chance to think, to make you look welcoming and for people to feel comfortable around you.

*** Stand tall and look the world straight in the eye**

Slouching can be mistaken as not caring and having a slovenly attitude. There is no need to stand with a ram rod military bearing but a person who stands tall has confidence in oneself as a person.

*** Grooming is essential**

How often do you see successful corporate people coming to work with greasy hair and smelling of a big physical workout? Never. If you don't take the time to care for yourself how will you be expected to take care of the work you are given or the company you represent?

* No one likes a bad smell

We all avoid bad smells. If you have bad breath, deal with it. If it is a medical condition you should treat it accordingly. Basic oral hygiene makes you more pleasant to be around. The same goes for the person who lives on coffee and cigarettes in the morning. You can end up with a very strong breath that you should treat with mints. (Breakfast and giving up smoking is a healthier alternative.)

* When in Rome

Do your research and discover how the other people in the office dress. Day one is not the time to exert your own stamp of individuality on the others. You want to look as if you have been there forever so everyone will feel comfortable around you.

* **Don't jump in where fools dread to tread**

  Day one at a new job and you want to get to know everyone and be known. Don't rush into making your choices. The first people you start hanging out with could be on the wrong ladder to your success and they may hold you back. Do your work and get to know everyone in time.

* **Everyone is terribly well suited**

  You have to wear a suit but look out for any colour and fun in the shirts and ties your colleagues are wearing. Putting this together successfully will have you standing out from the crowd. In *Getting Handsome* I have lots of tips for the successful combinations of shirts and ties.

* **Forget the suit; we are a casual bunch around here**

  These words can send a chill up any wardrobe. Business casual can be far trickier to wear than the usual corporate suit and tie. To look smart and professional, follow the clothing guidelines in 'Business casual' on page xx.

Get yourself ahead and act SMART

Once you have the position in a business, industry or group situation the following five points on being S–M–A–R–T will steer you towards becoming a pivotal and strong member through raising your credibility. For a person to be smart they are exhibiting a keen intellect, sharp thinking and a stylish mode of dressing. I thought it was a wonderful acronym for getting ahead.

Smile and greet everyone

It is important to greet everyone you come in contact with. Everyone has an opinion and the more people you are known to, the greater your star shall shine. Never presume yourself to be above anyone.

Make yourself known

You want to be *the* person everyone thinks of in relation to your area. You want to become the expert. This can happen by writing articles for your association, your company, your local newspaper, in-house newsletter and any other related industry magazines and papers. Getting your name in print will raise your profile and your credibility, and situate you as an expert.

Ask for feedback

The true professional is not afraid of critics. Asking for feedback will give you the advantage of knowing what you are a) doing well and b) could do better. Most people will appreciate the opportunity to give you what may turn out to be invaluable advice. A word of caution, this is not a platform for self-adulation: your critics can tell when your request for feedback is not genuine.

Respect yourself and others

It is important that you show respect to yourself as well as to those around you. Putting yourself down has the effect of giving you the martyr stance, where everyone has to refute what you say and bolster you up, which results in you appearing to have low self-confidence. It can also then give the necessary fuel to your detractors to bring you down. Never bring attention to your faults.

It is not necessary, nor is it wise, to badmouth colleagues or associates to others. If they are doing anything wrong it will come out eventually. I am a total believer in karma.

Take the time to get to know everyone

Today's assistant could be tomorrow's manager. As everyone knows, it is more often who we know, not what we know, that gets us through life. By taking the time to get to know the people you are associated with, it could surprise you how many doors open up to you, including doors you never knew existed.

* Corporate coiffure or surfie shag

Your hair is the first area people look at and it's an indicator of how you look. For men the corporate look is always short back and sides.

For women, have your hair no longer than shoulder length if you are wearing it out. If it is any longer, look into styles that allow you to put your hair up easily every day so that you don't have your long hair swinging around your shoulders.

*** Corporate cuts**

Men: you should have the back of your neck trimmed at least every three weeks. A shaggy neck isn't a good look. Women: look into having a trim at least every six weeks to ensure that your hair is in keeping with confident corporate look.

*** You can tell a person by the cut of their clothing**

By choosing quality clothing over quantity you will always set yourself ahead. People judge you on the style and quality of your clothing so you must make sure you start off with the right pieces.

*** Shine those shoes**

Have your shoes shined and clean; people will look at you and see whether you take enough care in yourself to decide whether you will take enough care with their company.

*** Lounging is for slobs**

In an initial assessment, people will look at how you hold yourself, your deportment, how well you stand, how well you sit. This is a time to stand up straight and look everyone in the eye. If you slouch you will be looked at as someone who lacks confidence in themselves and therefore maybe does not have the confidence to handle the job at hand.

corporate clothing

The perfect fit

Jackets

* Shoulders first

There is no point in buying a jacket that does not fit your shoulders. The fabric must lie flat between the shoulder blades without any pulling or puckering.

* Keep your lapels flat

The lapels of a jacket must lie flat against the fabric. If your lapels have a tendency to curl up you may want to take the jacket to a tailor to see if something can be done with the interfacing, or it might be that the jacket is too tight and is pulling. Flat lapels show that a jacket fits well.

*** Your jacket must close**

Do not wear a jacket that does not even do up. I have seen jackets worn that will still fit on the shoulders but due to a bulging girth no longer do up in the middle. Either have it let out or go and purchase a jacket that fits. When you present yourself to someone you must be able to do up your jacket as it will give you a professional finish.

*** Keep your vents closed**

The vent is the opening in the jacket that occurs at the bottom of the jacket to give you more movement. There may be a single vent in the rear of the jacket or smaller vents on the sides. Fashion and style will dictate what style of vents you have in your jacket but whichever the style, they must lie flat. If they have a tendency come open then once again the jacket does not fit and you are spelling out to everyone else that you have squeezed yourself into that jacket.

* **Lose the monkey arms**

Your jacket sleeve should finish more closely to the wrist than the knuckles. Ideally your jacket sleeve needs to finish one centimetre shorter than your shirt sleeve, whether you are male or female. The proper way to wear a jacket is so that your shirt sleeve shows through. In the case of a woman, when she is wearing a small camisole under a jacket then obviously there will be no shirt sleeve showing. Your jacket sleeve should finish just a centimetre or so below your wrist.

* **Shirts**

The first place that your shirt must fit you properly is around the neck. You don't want your neck to look as if it is swimming in the collar, nor do you want to look as if you are being squeezed into the collar. The test is to be able to slip two fingers in between your neck and your shirt collar.

Your shirt sleeves should be long enough to come out the end of your jacket, but you should not see any more than 1–1.5 cm of shirt cuff at the bottom of your sleeve. Any more than that and either your shirt sleeve is too long or your jacket sleeve is too short.

You will know if your shirt sleeve is too short if you can't bring your arm up into a right angle without your shirt cuff disappearing under your jacket. It should stay in the same position.

*** Wear a shirt where the collar suits your face**

There is quite a large section on this in *Getting Handsome;* essentially, you want a collar that will complement your features, not detract from them. Any good retailer or stylist will be able to help you with styles to suit you.

* Gaping is not acceptable

There are two areas where a shirt may gape. On a man with a rather large abdomen, his shirt may gape over his belly. This is not attractive and cannot be hidden with a tie. For women, you don't want gaping at your bust line. It will create a focal point and it is the last place you want to create a focus. Your aim is to keep the attention on your face, so wear a shirt where the fabric still lies flat when the buttons are done up.

Pants

* Watch your waist

For your pants to fit properly you need to be able to place two fingers in between you waistband and your body. Any more than that and you will end up with a paper bag finish, a style that was in fashion many years ago but not right now. Or, you will find yourself squeezed into your pants so that they will not sit flat, they will pull both front and rear. You will also be so uncomfortable you will be just dying to get them off by the end of the day.

* Ensure your pockets stay closed

Trousers that are too small will often pull the side pockets open. This is not only unflattering but is also a tricky situation if there are pickpockets around. Make sure your pants fit properly and that your pockets lie flat.

For women with pockets that are more decorative than functional, I would recommend having them stitched up. If you follow the initial stitching line, the pockets can be invisibly closed and no one need know whether the pockets work or not.

* Perfect pleats lie flat

Whether your pleats fold inwards or outwards they must lie flat. Pleats are designed as a style feature of clothing, not to allow you added room for growth. So if you are wearing a pair of trousers and the pleats have pulled so tight there is no longer a pleat in them it is time to upgrade to a larger pair of trousers.

* Keep your private bits private

Women need to ensure the front of their trousers are not too tight. There are some things that should remain hidden from view and too tight trousers can just make your anatomy a little bit too revealing.

The same goes for men: you do not want to be squeeze yourself into a pair of trousers that are so tight that all the crown jewels come to light. This is a time for decorum and for being quietly, corporately attired.

* **Perfect pants deserve the perfect length**

Women, aim to have your trousers fall all the way to the ground without any breaks such as creases at the ankle, and stop at the point the trousers touch the tops of your shoes.

For men, traditionally the trousers should only have one break or crease between the shoe and the bottom of the trouser. I have found though from working with men and dressing them, that in reality the trousers need to fall to the back of their shoes just above where the sole begins. This can lead to two creases at the front of the trousers, depending on the shoes. Anything shorter than this will have the trousers catching at the back of the shoes when walking.

* Long pants lead to ground focus

If your trousers are too long you will have a concertina effect at the bottom, with excessive folds created by sitting at the top of your shoes. You will also damage the back of your hem when you walk and inevitable wear and tear and pulled threads will occur. When your trousers are too long people will also notice it and spend the time focusing unintentionally on your feet. Don't have people looking at the floor: have them looking at your face. So get those trousers altered to the right length and dress like a polished professional.

Skirts

* Waist not, want not

Just as with a good pair of trousers, you need to be able to fit two fingers between the waistband of your skirt and your body. Any more and the skirt will end up sitting lower than your waist and further onto your hips; any tighter and you will end up with a 'muffin top' effect. This will be uncomfortable, and can be unsightly.

* A good split is vertical, not horizontal

Splits in skirts are there for two reasons: firstly as a design feature, and secondly, to allow you to move without the fabric being tight around your knees. It is important, however, to keep in mind that this split is a style design and at no point should you be wearing a skirt which is so tight that your split goes across the skirt, instead of up.

* **A little decorum, please**

  The ideal length for a corporate skirt should be no shorter than 2.5 cm above the knees. This is not to be prudish, but any shorter and your skirt may create too much of a stir in the office. This will take people's minds off the work you do and onto the things you do.

* **Comfort is important**

  Ensure your skirt has enough fabric and is not so tight that you can sit down comfortably in a meeting or all day at your desk without feeling that you have a vice around your waist and thighs.

* **Lining is for comfort, not display**

  Make sure that at no time the lining of your skirt is visible either through shrinkage in the fabric or having the back seam split.

* **Corporate skirts are straight, not curved**

Your work skirt needs to fall straight down from the back of your bottom, rather than coming in tightly around your thighs. Skirts that fit the body that snugly are better designed for evening and social activities rather than corporate or business attire.

Dresses

* **Keep some air in your clothing**

This is a favourite one of mine; not only does it make clothing fit well, it can also make you look slimmer. Dresses that are too tight have no place in the corporate market, and can also make you appear larger than you are. So a perfect dress for the corporate woman is one that will have a little bit of movement between the fabric and your flesh.

* Lose the ooze

Sleeveless dresses are okay in business as long as you have your jacket handy to wear for any time you may have to go into a meeting. Also, make sure that your flesh is not oozing out of the armholes. Once again, as with the tip before, you need to have a little bit of air in your clothes.

business traditional

*** The suit**

The suit is the basis of the traditional wardrobe favoured by many financial institutions, law firms and other industries that require an authoritative, credible, solid, respectable and reliable presence. It is the highest level of dressing and it is the one that will have you standing out in the corporate market.

*** Colour me corporate**

Traditional colours worn in the business suit are black, navy, grey and charcoal for both women and men. Women can wear some of the lighter colours in summer, such as cream and stone. Suits may be single- or double-breasted and the fabric can be plain, pin-striped, checked, or even have a very fine pattern through it to give a very subtle appearance to the fabric.

* Women: trousers are not true tradition

Unfortunately, trousers—as popular as they are—are still not considered a true traditional business suit for women. A true suit would generally have either a skirt or a dress as a partner to the jacket. Trousers are becoming more widely acceptable but if you are looking to join a new company, look at how the other women dress before you show up for an interview in a trouser suit. It might take away the edge that you are looking for.

* Blouses for women

In traditional business dress, blouses (as opposed to knits) are the only option. Keep in mind that if your blouse is sheer then you need your jacket to remain buttoned up at all times unless you are wearing a camisole underneath it.

✱ Traditional accessories for women

At all times hosiery must be worn. It needs to be sheer and in either a flesh tone, smoke or dark grey. Opaque hosiery will reduce the professionalism of this outfit.

Scarves are a wonderful addition to your wardrobe though for traditional business dress they must be a sheer or a satin fabric. Printed scarves with a small print or pattern in all colours will work. This is the perfect opportunity to add some femininity and colour into what can be quite a dark and sombre wardrobe in the traditional business style of dressing.

* Traditional shirts for men need not be boring

The shirts you wear with your suit are long sleeved. You can wear pastels or you might like to favour strong red or blue stripes on a white background. Some of you will have matching collars and cuffs; others may opt for a contrast of a white collar and cuff. You have the option of wearing a plain cuff or a French cuff with cufflinks. At all times you must wear a tie.

Remember that if you are wearing a double-breasted jacket, don't wear a shirt with a buttoned-down collar or walk with your jacket undone.

* Co-ordinating with your pants

You may choose to wear a smooth black leather belt that will match your shoes and in this instance black leather is the only coloured belt you will be wearing. Some Europeans like to go with the option of brown belts and brown shoes, however traditionalists in Australia still like the black leather belt with traditional business suit.

* **You also have the option of wearing braces**

  In this case a little more colour and individuality can come through and your braces will only be seen when you take your jacket off in a more relaxed setting. You can even match them to your tie.

* **Double ups don't work**

  Wearing braces is fine if you like that look, but never wear a belt with them if you want to dress properly.

* **Match your colours**

  At all times your socks need to match your belt so you will generally wear a dark plain or discreet pattern. Remember, no comics on your socks and make sure they are long enough to go past your calves and close to your knees. No one wants to see your hairy legs as you cross them in the middle of a meeting.

* Tired ties impress no one

Tie your tie properly to have a dimple at the base of the knot at your neck. The rest of your tie should lie flat and reach the belt on your trousers, or the waistline if you are wearing braces.

No matter how good or how expensive your tie was, once it starts fraying and looking shabby around the edges it needs to be replaced.

* Bow ties versus long ties

Traditional business dress can be worn with either a bow tie or a standard tie. The difference is the amount of personality you want to show and the amount of character and the style of person that you are. Bow ties are often favoured by lawyers, surgeons and other highly esteemed professions. Your tie is where much of your personality will come through. You can wear strong colours or light colours, but the colour you choose will depend on the impact you want to create. Once again, cartoon ties will only make a fool out of you.

* What your pocket says

To complete a business suit you can add a pocket handkerchief; this will say quite a bit about your personality. A well-pressed handkerchief is very formal and precise whilst a loosely draped handkerchief will have you looking more flamboyant and creative.

* Accessories are the little touches that add timeless appeal

Your accessories need to be as elegant as your outfit; therefore your ideal colour combinations for watches, earrings or any other accessories you may choose for jewellery needs to be understated, timeless and elegant. The ideal to wear is either white or gold metals as well as precious and semi-precious stones. Ideal watchbands are either gold or silver, or you may choose to wear a fine black leather band.

Business classic

* **It does not need to be traditional**

  The business classic side of dressing is for the person who wants to look professional and dependable, organised and conscientious, with an orientation to detail without looking too dominant and too precise in their dressing. This style is probably the most common of all styles in the Australian corporate market as it is still a suit, yet with a more relaxed finish.

* **Classic times**

  The best times to wear business classic is when you want to present a more formal and powerful image at a first meeting with the client. It is recommended when you are making presentations, leading a meeting or as the presenter at a trade show.

You can afford to allow more colour into your wardrobe. You may wish to incorporate some of the more contemporary colours of brown, olive green and aubergine for your suits.

* Classic clothing

The defining piece in your wardrobe is your jacket; at any time you wish to present yourself at this level of dress you must always wear one. Whilst classic dress is generally a suit, you can wear co-ordinated casuals as long as you are wearing a jacket.

* **Classic women**

You have the option here of wearing dresses, skirts or pants. Fabrics can be either structured or unstructured, the best being wool, linen, silk blends, light- to medium-weight wool blends as well as micro fibres. For tops you can choose between blouses, camisoles or twin sets in silk or cotton. You may also wish to wear to some fine turtleneck or crewneck jumpers that are a fine enough weave to allow a jacket to be worn over the top.

* **Classic men**

As stated above, the main piece of the classic wardrobe is the jacket. You can choose a suit, but in this case you would want your suit to be in a less traditional fabric; otherwise go for a blazer or sports coat over your trousers. Shirts can be solid or patterned but should always be long sleeved. You may opt to wear the polo style of long-sleeved top.

Jumpers may be worn as long as they are in a light enough material that will allow for a jacket to be worn over the top.

* Classic accessories for women

Once again, hosiery is a must. This time you can wear semi sheers as well as the sheers and opaques; in fact the sheerer the stocking the more traditional your style of clothing will appear. Trouser socks can be worn in colours to match your hemline and shoes. Scarves can be bolder and brighter in woven knits of silk or wool. Your jewellery can have a lot more life to it and you might choose large pieces. As well as gold, silver and pearls you may choose ivory, onyx or jade.

* Classic men's accessories

Socks are important, but you can wear more elaborate patterns. However, don't go for the comics and stick to basically corporate.

* **Remember to keep in mind these final points**

You must always wear a jacket. Keep clothing and your accessories at the same level. If you dress to the traditional style you will need to wear traditional accessories; for a classic style you can relax everything just a little.

business casual

*** Keep it smart, not relaxed**

This level of dressing can be one of the trickiest levels to carry off successfully. Once they know they don't have to wear their suit or jacket to work, many men and women end up looking way too relaxed in their style of dressing for the job. The introduction of casual Friday can create an even greater degree of confusion. Casual dressing does not mean jeans and T-shirts. That style of dressing should only be for your time outside of work. It does not fit into the corporate market.

* Casual women

In this instance a jacket is not a prerequisite. The guidelines to keep in mind for work are that your clothing should look professional. It should not be too short, too tight or too sporty. So where does that leave you? Try smart trousers, crisp shirts, fine knits and always closed-toe shoes.

* Casual men

The best way to describe what is acceptable is to cover what is not appropriate. Any clothing that would work in the following situations generally won't do at work: sports and workout clothing, beach wear, surfing accessories, hiking clothes and night-club apparel. What does that leave you with? Casual flat-front and pleated trousers in anything but denim, long- and short-sleeved buttoned shirts, fine knit jumpers and lace-up or slip-on leather shoes

* Wardrobe basics

Starting a new job is not only daunting but can also be expensive. However, you can look great every day without spending a fortune. The following outlines will give you enough pieces to allow you to have a different outfit on every day for a minimum of three months for men and four months for women.

Women

Your basic wardrobe will consist of:

2 jackets (one in each colour)

3 pairs of pants

2 skirts

3 short-sleeved tops (ones that can be worn on their own as well as under a shirt)

3 long-sleeved blouses or shirts

Basic accessories

2 pairs of court shoes in core or neutral colour (If your core colour is burgundy, green or even red you might find co-ordinating shoes in the same colour difficult. I suggest a neutral in black or a shade of brown to make a match.)

1 pair of trouser shoes in core or neutral colour (Again the same rules as for the court shoes apply here.)

1 handbag in smooth leather that will co-ordinate with the shoes

Men

These guidelines will have you looking your best both in business and in the community. Your wardrobe should consist of:

1 suit
1 sports coat or blazer
2 jumpers
4 pairs of trousers
6 shirts— long-sleeved and either business or casual
2 polo tops
2 pairs leather lace-up shoes

Aside from the polo tops, if your wardrobe was to consist of those 16 items you would have 96 outfits to wear to work. That does not even allow for the extra combinations ties can bring. The addition of another jacket will alone create another 24 variations for you.

colour your world

The colours you wear will have a strong impact on the people you are talking to. Ensure you are wearing the right colours to get the right psychological message across to the people you are dealing with.

Black

Positives: Dignified, cosmopolitan, mysterious and firm

Negatives: Solemn, antagonistic, arrogant and proud

Best impact

- In contrast with another colour
- To keep people at a distance
- In the evening to play it safe or sexy
- To show respect at a Western funeral

When to avoid

- If you want someone to open up to you
- At a wedding
- Near your face, unless you have the colouring to handle it

White

Positives: Pure, immaculate and modern

Negatives: Clinical, uninteresting and bland

Best impact

- White has a strong association with traditional medicine so it will impart impeccable hygiene standards if worn as a coat
- To create a strong contrast against darker colours
- As an all-over, attention-grabbing progressive image
- To show respect at an Eastern funeral

When to avoid

- If you have minimal time for personal grooming
- As a complete outfit in the evening unless close to the equator
- In grubby urban areas where it will require regular washing

Red

Positives: Passionate, energetic and optimistic

Negatives: Opinionated, bold and impertinent

Best impact

- When you want to be recognised
- To give an artificial boost of energy when mildly tired
- To project authority without being threatening; wear it as an accent with a moderate contrast

When to avoid

- If you are overtired or overstressed as it will only heighten the mood
- When you want to stay in the background
- Chairing a meeting where you want there to be a flow of ideas

Blue

Positives: Composed, scrupulous, reliable, dependable

Negatives: Safe, orthodox, exact

Best impact

- The deepest of blues convey authority
- On television, mid blues are very media friendly
- It is the world's favourite colour and the easiest colour to wear

When to avoid

- Making a creative pitch
- At a conference of bankers, lawyers and accountants unless you want to blend in
- Whenever you want to project success and confidence

Brown

Positives: Friendly, welcoming and receptive

Negatives: Mundane, insecure and pragmatic

Best impact

- To get people to open up and communicate more freely
- Women should wear it in a rich shade

When to avoid

- Not really a good colour for the corporate male wardrobe
- Positioning for a management takeover
- When meeting friends with problems—you'll cop the lot
- When wanting to attract attention

Pink

Positive: Delicate, sympathetic and feminine

Negative: Trivial, insignificant and sissy

Best impact

- To soften an austere business suit
- As grandmother of the bride
- When petitioning in a divorce court. Even his attorney will feel sorry for you. *Sorry, men!*

When to avoid

- Discussing a promotion
- At a client dinner, the only pink women should wear is their lipstick
- Any time you want to be taken seriously

Yellow

Positive: Animated, carefree and vivacious

Negative: Fickle, skittish and unstable

Best impact

- To cheer yourself up
- When working with children
- Best as a jacket if you want to be recognised in a crowd

When to avoid

- In a business meeting if you don't have anything to contribute
- When asking for an overdraft
- If you live in a sunny climate as it can radiate

Green

Positive: Strong, persistent and reliable

Negative: Obstinate, resolute and rebellious

Best impact

- After days of more flamboyant colours it will bring you down to earth
- When you are over-stressed and over tired it is calming
- If you work for an environmental company

When to avoid

- When fund-raising
- As a rallying colour— it doesn't project new ideas
- As an entrepreneur you will not stand out from the crowd and you want your ideas to be taken seriously

Orange

Positives: Animated, dynamic and creative

Negatives: Shallow, flighty and volatile

Best impact

- If you want to be seen in the dark or you need to be visible
- If you work behind the scenes and want to energise yourself
- In measured doses if it suits your colouring
- Burnt orange has broken through the barriers and has become a fashionable and acceptable colour to wear

When to avoid

- For business of any kind, it is the least professional colour
- When you are on a diet as it will make you act impulsively
- When you want to look elegant: on the wrong person it looks cheap

Violet

Positives: Unique, perceptive and serene

Negatives: Juvenile, uninterested and pre-occupied

Best impact

- Mid–deep tones: to project confidence and individuality
- Great on television, provided it is not too dark
- On occasions requiring diplomacy

When to avoid

- When a low-key, reassuring profile is called for
- When you are depressed
- When you need to project stability and security

Grey

Positives: Reputable, calm and harmonious

Negatives: Unexceptional, adequate and detached

Best impact

- In business— grey is a great option for suits, less authoritarian yet still smart
- Team up with a strong accent to project innovation
- For a job interview with a smart white shirt to play it safe

When to avoid

- In the creative sectors
- When you need to be a catalyst
- On any occasion when you need to be noticed

corporate clothing disasters

* **Shorts**

  Shorts may show off your great legs but are not going to do anything for your credibility.

* **Sports clothing**

  Unless you are attending a sports day there is no excuse for going to work in your gym gear or your tennis, golf, football or any other sports clothing.

* **Avoid the midriff**

  You may have a flat stomach and an amazing figure, but showing off your midriff is not doing your corporate presentation any favours.

*** Moccasins or mini skirts**

Both of these can be disastrous to your career. Remember: wear good shoes, clothing that covers and don't expose too much flesh.

maintenance

Ironing your shirt

A badly ironed shirt looks dreadful, so remember these basic ironing tips next time you are pressing your shirt.

* **Collar first**

  Start with the underside of the collar; work out towards the ends and back to the centre.

* **Shoulder yoke**

  Smooth the yoke by slipping one shoulder over the narrow end of the board, ironing from the shoulder to the centre of the back. Repeat on the other side. Alternatively you can work from the inside of your shirt and iron across the yoke.

✱ Cuffs

Iron the inside first, then the outside. The same goes for a French cuff.

✱ Sleeves

Iron the body of each sleeve, beginning with the cuff and ironing towards the shoulder, and then do the reverse side.

✱ Body

Begin with the front panels of the shirt and finish across the back.

✱ And back to the collar

Once the whole shirt is done, re-press the top of the collar.

Ironing tips that professionals use

In the last rinse of washing, add half a cup of salt. This will assist greatly in ironing.

Place aluminium foil under your ironing-board cover. This will reflect the heat to the underside of the garment and will basically iron both sides at the same time.

When the iron is cold, clean the face with tooth paste. This cleans any build-up and will make the iron glide more smoothly. Touching the metal part of the iron from time to time whilst ironing will reduce static build up and will make the iron last longer. Just don't burn yourself.

On the inner side of trouser pleats and leg creases, gently rub a small candle, and then iron the outer, or correct, side. This will give you a more defined and professionally pressed crease.

Always iron lengthwise as circular strokes can stretch your fabric. For tough wrinkles use the burst of steam.

Tie

* **Avoid the drycleaners**

  While dry cleaners may be able to remove spots, once they press a tie, they will compress the lining and dull the lustre of the silk. A water stain is easily removed by rubbing the tie with a similar piece of fabric (try the other end of the tie). Stains of a more serious nature can often be removed with a spot remover such as carbon tetrachloride.

  Don't stay in knots

  Always take the knot out of the tie. This will help avoid permanent creasing.

*** Pulling your tie apart stretches it**

Remove your tie by undoing it the way you did it up. Pulling the smaller end through the knot causes the tie to stretch out of shape.

*** Roll your ties**

Ties which tend to stretch can be gently rolled and stored in a drawer. Don't put them on clothes hangers as they will slip off and/or twist.

*** Clip it, don't pull it**

Never pull loose threads as this can cause permanent damage. Clipping the threads as close as possible to the fabric will give your tie extra life.

*** Don't try to kill your tie**

Avoid choking the tie knot as this tends to twist the lining.

✱ Colours can run

Before applying any water, test your tie in an inconspicuous area as some dyes may bleed.

✱ Blot the spot

Do not attempt to rub away stains as this may cause fabric abrasion and colour loss. Only blot the spotted area.

✱ Let it steam

If ties are badly wrinkled, steam them; do not iron them. Ironing will compress the lining, flattening the tie and causing the material to shine.

✱ Chemicals can discolour

Keep aftershaves and colognes well away as their chemicals damage the colour of ties.

*** Let it rest**

Alternate your ties to not only give them a break but also provide a break to everyone who looks at you. Your tie will come back to shape after lying rolled up in your drawer.

travel tips

* **Use your layers**

Layer the bottom of your case with all crushable items to build up a flat base.

* **Keep your trousers flat**

Lay your trousers together over the flat base so that half the length of the trousers is in the case and the remainder is hanging out of the case. Fill in the rest of the case and, before closing, fold in the rest of your trousers so they are never quite folded in half.

* **Dry-cleaning bags are a godsend**

Pack your shirts in dry-cleaning bags to minimise the need to iron. Dry cleaning bags can be the traveller's best friend. They reduce many wrinkles that a suitcase can create in your garments.

* Three simple steps to packing a jacket

If you don't have a suit-pack, follow these guidelines:

1 Lay your jacket flat in your case with the hem against one end of your suitcase.

2 Fold the arms flat across the body of your jacket.

3 To make it fit, fold your jacket closest to the shoulders. Ironing and your body heat will take care of any wrinkles that may occur.

* Suit packs save you time

You won't have the hassles of having to re-iron everything when you get to your destination.

* Keep it dry

Invest in a wet pack. Carry all shampoos and skin care in small travelling bottles, inside a wet pack. This will save you from having a major blow-out when a bottle leaks in your bag.

* **Plan your wardrobe options**

  Pack clothing which co-ordinates. This way if one item is soiled you can replace it quickly with another top or bottom without having to carry a whole second outfit.

* **Don't trust it all in the hold**

  Keep all the important pieces on you. Pack your travel documents, money and important medicines in your carry-on bag—losing your luggage, no matter how long for, will not be a complete disaster.

* **Keep spares on hand**

  Don't try to remember it all. If you travel often, keep your toilet bag permanently packed. You don't want to get to your destination only to realise you have left your toothbrush, toothpaste or deodorant behind.

*** Samples save space**

Try out those samples. Gather all of the skin and hair-care samples you find in magazines and save them for your travel bag. They will save space and can be thrown out as they are used up.

*** When travelling, pack two jackets**

It will allow one to air whilst you wear the other and it gives you a variety of looks.

*** Ties extend a travelling wardrobe considerably**

A change of tie can completely transform your outfit and your look. It is a very simple way to appear to have an extensive wardrobe, even if you do keep wearing the same suit.

* Accessories can change your look

Women, you can spend all day in your meeting in a little black dress with sheer stockings, small earrings and a fine gold chain. When it is time to go out, lose the hosiery, slip on a strappy pair of evening shoes and glitz up the jewellery. It is a new you without a complete extra wardrobe.

* Wool and cotton travel well

When deciding what to pack for that business conference or simply a trip away, you will find wool and cotton the easiest to travel with. Polyester travels well but doesn't breathe well, nor does it look too smart, and linen will just end up a pile of wrinkles.

* **Patterns have more variety**

A patterned shirt will give your wardrobe greater variety. Your patterned shirt can be worn with ties to meetings during the day and without your tie for a more casual look at night without looking traditionally dressed down.

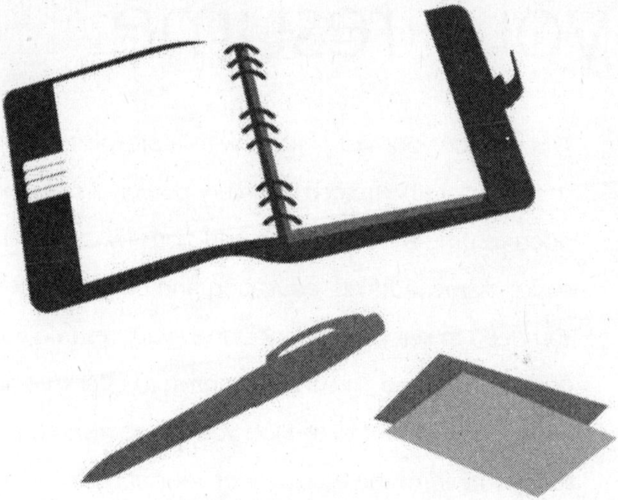

surviving interviews

your resume

This may be your first contact with a prospective employer so it needs to be treated as a very powerful sales tool. A good resume is not too long and starts by covering the basics: name, address, education and employment history. You need to sell yourself. Include in your resume your qualifications and skills that you have to offer that are especially pertinent to the job you are applying for. Make sure you inform the employer of your potential and value to their company.

interview techniques

Preparation

- Do your homework on the company.
- See how they dress—appear at the interview looking as if you fit in immediately. Don't make them guess how you will look.
- Discover what their grooming standards are. Adhere to their grooming standards in how you present yourself at your interview.
- Research their hours of operation so you can ask relevant questions pertaining to your own schedule.
- Find any other points of relevance to the position you are after that you might like to ask about.

The interview

- Arrive 5 minutes early.
- Shake hands with all who are interviewing and wait to be asked to be seated.
- Maintain good posture and eye contact.
- Make positive references to past employers and situations.
- Be clear on your career goals.
- If a question is not clear ask for clarification.
- At the end of the interview, shake hands with everyone again as you leave.
- If, after the interview, you felt the job was for you, send a letter of thanks to whoever interviewed you for the chance to meet. This can be a very powerful tool.

Target selection

This style of interview is used to find specific qualities in an individual. The formula is to ask situational questions to which you give a specific scenario answer from experience and often back that up with what you learnt or what you could have done better.

Example questions

* Communication questions

- Tell me about a time when you had a conflict with someone in a work group. How did you resolve it, what was the outcome?
- What is the most important report you have written? Who was it written for and what was your feedback?
- Describe a tough situation where you had to get information from people to make a tough decision. What was challenging about it? How well did you do?

* Attention to detail

How do you ensure your work is free from errors? Tell me about a time you made a significant error. What did you do?

* Initiative

Tell me about a time when you went over and above the call of duty.

* Leadership

Have you ever been in a position where you have had to assign work to others? How did you do this? What follow-up measures did you use to ensure the work was done?

* Decision making

What is the most difficult work-related decision you have ever had to make? What other options did you consider?

*** Flexibility / Adaptability**

Tell me about a time when you had to adjust quickly to changes in priorities. How did this affect you? What did you do specifically to manage the situation?

*** Time management**

From time to time we all find ourselves a bit behind on some task. Tell me about a time when you fell really behind time. Why did this happen? What did you do to correct the situation? What was the outcome of your efforts to catch up? How often has this happened in the past two years?

*** Other standard questions**

- Give an example of a time when you did not agree with an employer or supervisor.
- Are you able to work overtime?
- What qualities can you bring to this position?
- What qualifications do you have for this position?

- Can you give me an example of something you did well this year?
- Why did you leave your last position?
- What are your strengths?

dining with dignity

* From breakfast to buffet

It is great that you got to the position you now hold. But do you know your paté from your pinot, or crudités from your crustaceans? Knowing dining etiquette will save you from getting lost amongst your cutlery and allow you to save face at any restaurant.

* Remember 'Pretty Woman'

The first thing to remember as you are looking at all the cutlery in front of you is to work from the outside in. So if you are trying to work out which knife and fork to use, the ones furthest out are the first you pick up. In the event that the table is fully laden and you haven't ordered an entrée, the waiting staff will normally take away the cutlery that is no longer required.

* Navigating your cutlery

The forks sit on the left of the plate and are used in the left hand. Knives and spoons sit on the right of the plate and are used in the right hand.

* Bread and butter is on the left

This refers to your bread and butter plate. Have you ever been at a function where the bread rolls are already set out and you didn't know which one was yours? The easiest way is to remember that the roll is on your left and you will hold it in your left hand as you apply the butter with your knife which is in your right hand.

*** Never cut a roll**

Always, always break your roll: the knife is only for applying the butter. Generally there is a pat of butter in a bowl in front of you on the table. Take your bread and butter knife, which sits on your bread and butter plate, and take as much butter as you think you will need to butter your entire piece of bread. Put this butter onto the side of your plate and, as you break off a piece of bread, use the butter which is already on your plate so that you don't continually have to lean over into the central pat of butter.

*** Solids to your left and liquids to your right**

Solids, like bread, go on the left. Liquids— your wine glass, water glass and coffee—all sit, hopefully not all at once, in front of your right hand.

* Try a little of everything

If you have been invited out to a corporate function and the food seems foreign to you, at least try a little of everything on your plate. It could be that your host is from a foreign country and has decided to favour you by offering you the specialities of their country. I remember once at a favourite Japanese restaurant where the owners had come to know us quite well, they gave us a dish that was highly sought after and a delicacy in Japan. It was not to my liking (let's just leave it at that!) but we at least tried a little so that we did not insult our hosts.

* A napkin is for your lap; it's not a table decoration

Within a few seconds of sitting down, or once everyone is seated, place your napkin on your lap so that if at any time during the meal you spill or dribble anything, it will land in your napkin. At the same time, if anything is on your fingers you can discreetly clean them under the table rather than have everyone witness the mess you are in.

* Compliments to the host

If you are invited to dinner at someone's house, always remember to compliment the host and the magnificent meal. If you are having trouble complimenting the host on their magnificent meal, you can always compliment them on their house or the presentation of the meal or even the time it has taken them to prepare it. Always remember that it is a special privilege to have been invited so thank them for the privilege.

*** Toast the host—don't get toasted**

The first toast is generally given by the host. Raise your glass and take a sip. In the event there are multiple toasts being given, remember you can toast with soft drink or water to save you the embarrassment of finding yourself completely inebriated by the end of the evening.

*** Never toast yourself**

If you are the object of the toast, when everyone else is drinking from their glass as a toast to you, you do not take part in the drinking.

*** Loose lips sink ships**

You will be taken out by clients or your bosses for meetings or celebrations. When alcohol is served there is no need to drink yourself into an unintelligible mess.

* **Keep your belongings off the table**

The table is a place for food and drinks. It is not the place to sit your mobile phone, your keys or your handbag. They should be left in your pocket or under your seat.

* **Never pick your teeth at the table**

If you have something in your teeth don't grab a business card, your knife or any other implement on the table to try to ply it out. Excuse yourself and go to the bathroom to remove whatever object may be jammed there. In the event there are tooth picks on the table, as in some Asian restaurants, it is polite to take a tooth pick and remove yourself to the bathroom rather than picking your teeth at the table as others may be doing.

*** Don't talk with your mouth full**

This is an oldie but a goodie. No matter who you are with or how important the information is you wish to get across, if you need to speak quickly, indicate with your hands that you are about to speak, finish what you are eating and then speak.

*** Keep your mouth shut**

Even today I see people who insist on eating with their mouth open. I don't know whether they are trying to savour the food more or they have never been taught the basic art of eating with their mouth closed.

*** Remember what a knife and fork are for**

I have witnessed a patron spearing a large piece of veal with a fork and waving it in the air. Positively feudal it appeared to me. Cut your food into bite-sized pieces and put it straight into your mouth.

* **Whatever hits the floor stays there**

  If you drop a knife, fork or anything else onto the floor whilst in a restaurant, leave it there and allow a waiter to pick it up for you and bring you a fresh implement.

* **Knives and forks are not an extension of a conversation**

  When you have something to say, place your knife and fork down on your plate with the tines of the fork down so that the waiters will know you are still eating. Never use them as part of your conversation; they are not a dagger to wield around.

* **Wait to be seated**

  In the event you have been invited out to a formal dinner party, wait until the host indicates where they would like you to sit so that you don't upset the plans for the table.

*** It's nice to say thank you**

After you have been invited to a cocktail party or any dining event it is always nice to send a hand-written 'thank you' to the host within 24 hours. It is these little touches that set you apart from the rest.

*** Taste your food before you season it**

It is the height of rudeness, upon receiving your meal, to cover it in salt and pepper before you even know what it tastes like. You are insulting both the host and the chef by not bothering to taste your food first to see it has been flavoured accordingly.

*** It is not a crime to say no to wine**

If you are attending a day-time function, or you don't drink alcohol, or you don't feel like any wine with the meal, when the waiter comes around to pour the wine don't turn your glass upside down, just place your hand over the top of it to indicate that you do not want any.

* How it goes in is how it comes out

In the event you need to remove something from your mouth, use the same implement to remove it as was used to put it in your mouth. In the instance of hand-held items such as small pieces of fruit, olives or nuts, you may remove the item with your fingers into a napkin. In the event of a dish where the item has gone in by a spoon, put it back onto the spoon before you put it in the napkin or on the side of your plate. The only exception is fish bones which will have entered your mouth via a fork but you may need your fingers to remove them.

* Who pays the bill?

It is generally courteous, if you have invited someone out for lunch, and have never done so before, to pay the bill. When you are hosting the function, you may wish to make arrangements with the restaurant before the meal is served, to pay with your credit card, so the bill is not brought to the table.

✱ Cocktail food

Always hold items of food in your left hand so that you have your right hand free to shake hands with those you may meet at a cocktail party.

✱ Never double dip

In the event there are crudités or vegetables being served with dips and sauces, only ever dip the item you are eating once. To double dip is strictly forbidden.

✱ Those pits

Olive pits don't get spat into the nearest pot plant or dropped back into the olive bowl. Keep them in your napkin or the bowl provided for the olive pits.

✱ Know your stems

When you are drinking red wine you hold the bowl of the glass, yet when you are drinking white wine you hold it by the stem so as not to warm the wine.

* Finessing the fork

A fork is not a shovel. There are times when you can use it upright, for example when eating a chilli or a curry or a risotto, but normally when using a fork push your food or spear it onto the fork and place it in your mouth with the tines facing down. If you are eating soft vegetables, press them onto the back of the fork before placing it in your mouth.

* Forks are not only for the left hand

Occasionally you will be served a meal such as spaghetti or, as I mentioned before, a chilli, curry or risotto. It is quite acceptable to eat it with your fork in your right hand and use it in a shovel-type motion. You will generally find if you are in a restaurant that the waiter will move your cutlery around to indicate this style. Occasionally with spaghetti you will also receive a soup spoon which you use to assist with twisting your spaghetti onto your fork. It takes a little practice but saves your spaghetti from flicking all over your face.

* Left-handed options

The only time it is okay to swap your knife and fork around is if you are left-handed and you have not managed to navigate your meal with your fork in your left hand and knife in your right. As long as you still use your knife and fork in the manner that they are customarily used, this is quite acceptable at the table.

* Don't grasp it like a club

Learn how to hold your knife and fork properly: between your thumb and forefinger with the rest of your fingers tucked against your hand. Some people make the mistake of grasping their utensils as if they are a weapon to be wielded around the dinner table. Not since the barbarians have we closed our fists over our knife or fork.

* Slurp your soup—sometimes

The soup spoon is more rounded in shape than a dessert spoon. To eat your soup, rather than bringing your spoon straight towards you and risking the dribbles going across your lap, spoon into your bowl away from you, touching the bottom of your spoon on the outer edge of your bowl to remove any last dribbles. In the event your soup is served in a bowl with handles, drink most of it with a soup spoon and you may pick up the bowl by the handles and drink the last bits. Many Asian restaurants will give you a bowl without handles but with very steep sides; once again, especially in the Japanese culture, the soup can be drunk directly from the bowl and in this instance slurping is not only considered acceptable but is the norm.

*** Elbows off**

At no time should your elbows be on the table. The only exception would be when having coffee with a friend and involved in a close conversation or in the evening if there are just the two of you at the table and you want to lean in and speak more privately.

*** Leave the cleaning up to the staff**

You are not at home, so there is no need to start stacking the plates once everyone has finished. If you are in a restaurant, that is the job of the waiting staff.

*** Finessing in the finger bowl**

Whenever you are at a seafood restaurant and you are eating crab or shelling prawns you will find a finger bowl placed on the table. It is there for everyone to dip their fingers in once they have finished eating and then clean them on their napkin.

* Don't confuse the waiters

If you are still eating your meal and are in the middle of a conversation, lay your knife and fork across each other on your plate with the tines down and the waiters will know you are still eating. If you have finished, place your knife and fork together either on the side of your plate or down the centre with the tines of your fork facing up and the sharp edge of the knife facing inwards: the waiters will know you have finished your meal.

* Wait for the waiter

Waiters are trained to serve your meals and clear up afterwards but it helps if you have an idea of what to expect. Your meal will be served to you from the left and cleared away from the right. Serving platters will also be offered to you from the left. So basically, food comes in on the left and leaves on the right.

*** A fishy situation**

If you are served an entire fish, you may find you are given a fish knife and fork. This cutlery looks different. It is wider, the fork has flatter tines and the knife is a different shape to a regular knife. Both the fork and knife are designed this way to make it easier to remove the bones from the fish rather than having to turn the fish over. In some Asian countries it is considered bad luck to turn a fish over.

*** Pick the pace up**

I was at a luncheon once and one of the guests took so long to eat their entree I had to leave before the main meal arrived. Keep up the pace with everyone else, don't get caught in a conversation so that everyone else is waiting for you to finish before they can move on.

*** Don't blow out at the buffet**

Yes, all the food may look fantastic but there is no need to pile your plate so high it looks as if you are eating for three.

* Keep your fork out of my food

If you are in a restaurant where everyone is sharing from the same dish it is fine to use the implements provided to put some food onto your own plate. However, it is completely inappropriate to lean over and spear your fork into someone else's meal without asking. Firstly, it is a sign of ownership and you could quite easily offend someone and secondly, it is highly offensive to just help yourself to someone else's food.

food handling with finesse

*** Artichokes**

Artichokes are eaten with your fingers. They may be served hot or cold and you eat them leaf by leaf, starting from the outside leaf, pulling off each leaf and scraping the flesh off the leaf with your teeth. Generally you won't have a side plate so you just build up a pile of discarded leaves on the side of your own plate. Once you have reached the heart of the artichoke, you finish it with a knife and fork.

* Asparagus

If asparagus is served as an entrée with dressing on the side or a little on the tips of the asparagus, you may pick it up in your fingers and slowly work your way down the asparagus until you get to the thicker end which is crunchy and stringy. You don't eat this part: leave it on the side of your plate. In the event the asparagus is served as a vegetable with your main course, eat it with your knife and fork.

* Avocado

If you have an avocado as an entrée maybe with seafood or a salad dressing, eat it with a small spoon. Avocado that comes sliced as part of a salad is eaten with a fork.

*** Oysters**

There are two ways of eating oysters. Natural oysters, to which you add sauce if you wish, come with their own small set of cutlery. Use the fork to dip the oyster into the sauce and then swallow whole. With oysters that come with their own dressing in the shell, you can use the fork to ensure that the oyster is not attached to the shell and then use the shell to slide the oyster into your mouth, allowing you to enjoy all of the dressing. This is one of the easiest ways to eat Oysters Kilpatrick as you get to enjoy all of the flavours of the bacon and the sauces. In the case of Oysters Mornay you may want to use the spoon to enjoy the creamy sauce that will be left in the shell.

* **Caviar**

If you are at a function where caviar is served you may need to prepare a piece for yourself. The caviar will have a serving spoon in the bowl; take a piece of the toast that will be served with it and use the serving spoon to put a small amount onto the toast and then maybe add some of the accompaniments that are being offered such as onions, eggwhites or lemon slices.

* **Cheese**

If a cheese platter is being passed around, use the cheese knives provided with the cheese to cut your own small slices and place them on your side plate. Help yourself to some crackers and enjoy the cheese away from the cheese board. If you don't have a spare knife then cut the cheese into small pieces so it is easier to put onto the crackers.

* Mussels

Mussels are often served with a fork, or you may even use another mussel shell as pincers to pull the remaining mussels from the shells. If the shell is not open, don't try to prise it open; place this mussel into the shell bowl and ignore. The same goes for clams. Generally there will be a bowl for the shells as well as a finger bowl.

* Corn on the cob

There are two accepted methods of eating corn. One is by putting little corn cob holders into the ends of the corn, dipping it in butter and eating it fresh off the cob. This is fun but very messy. If you are at a civilised dinner, you may wish to place the corn on its side, hold it at one end and slice the corn off the cob with your knife. You then eat the corn as you would your peas.

* Figs

Fresh figs don't appear that often. Eat them with a knife and fork if served as an entrée or with a fork and spoon if served as a dessert. The only area of a fig that you don't eat is the stem.

* Lobster and crayfish

These are a delicacy but also very messy. Be prepared to dive in, hands and all. Hopefully the lobster will be served cut in half and you can then use your fork to pull the flesh out of the main body. You will be given nut crackers and seafood forks (which are very long with two claws on the end). Use the nut crackers to break the shell of the legs and claws and then use the seafood fork to pull the flesh out. Be prepared to get messy and continue to use that fingerbowl. This is the only occasion where it is acceptable to tuck your napkin in at your neck.

*** Paté**

Paté may be served at a cocktail party, where you help yourself using a paté knife to spread it onto crackers. If it is an entrée or appetizer you will have your own individual serve of paté with a small knife and generally small square toasts. To serve the paté, smear a small amount onto your toast and enjoy it with your fingers. There is no need to use a knife and fork in this instance.

Dos and don'ts of the Chinese restaurant

*** Learn how to use chopsticks**

Chopsticks can be fiddly and if you haven't mastered the art and are out with clients for the first time it is perfectly acceptable to ask for a knife and fork rather than making yourself uncomfortable. If you are using chopsticks, expect to keep the same chopsticks for the entire meal. Place them on the chopstick holder which is part of your setting on the table.

* **Hand towels**

At the start and end of a meal at a good Chinese restaurant you will be presented with either a hot or cold hand towel. This is for your hands alone. It is not something to have a mini bath with. I have seen occasions where faces, necks and even arms are cleaned with the towel.

* **Chopsticks are used for eating, not talking**

As with all utensils, put your chopsticks down when you are talking. They are not an extension of your hand to help get a message across. It can be the same as pointing aggressively at a person.

* **Don't wave your chopsticks over the food**

Whilst you are making up your mind what you feel like eating, keep your chopsticks on your plate. They have been in your mouth and no one wants to see them being waved around the communal dish.

✱ Up-end your chopsticks

If you are going to use your chopsticks to take a piece out of a communal dish on the table, use the end that has not been in your mouth. That way people do not feel as though you are double dipping into their meal.

✱ Don't leave your chopsticks standing upright in a bowl

Traditionally in China a bowl is left on a coffin or grave as an offering with the chopsticks standing upright in the rice. To do the same in a Chinese restaurant is frowned upon.

✱ Slurping, snorting and belching is okay

The Chinese and many other Asian nationals make many noises when eating as a way of showing their enjoyment. It is perfectly acceptable and in fact is considered a compliment to be heard to make a lot of noise when you eat.

*** It is not necessary to empty your bowl**

In a banquet situation, if you empty your bowl the host may feel you have not had enough to eat. This is one instance where it is fine to leave food on your plate.

*** Mess means a good time**

Once walking through Singapore after one of their festivals I noticed tables left with food scraps all over them. I have since discovered that a messy table means a lot of fun has been had at that meal and everyone enjoyed themselves. So if you are dining out at a Chinese restaurant, short of throwing your food around, do not be concerned if you do spill the odd noodle.

Japanese restaurant rules

* Bare those feet

In a traditional Japanese restaurant you will be expected to remove your shoes before entering. Please do so, and leave them pointing away from the door.

* Chopsticks in Japan

The use of chopsticks in Japan is somewhat similar to China in that you don't spear your rice or use them to go rummaging around in the communal dishes. Japanese chopsticks are more finely pointed than Chinese chopsticks. Apparently, the higher up you hold your chopstick the more educated you are.

* Sushi with style

Sushi can be eaten with your hands. The best way to do so is to pick up a piece of sushi, turn it over so that the topping is dipped into the sauce, and then bite a piece off as it goes into your mouth. If you dip it into the sauce with the rice facing downwards you can end up with all the rice sitting in the sauce bowl.

* Never pour your own drink

In Japan and China it is considered polite to pour for other people, just as it is polite to serve other people their meal and then let someone serve and pour for you.

* Eyes up for a toast

Whenever someone toasts you or you are clinking glasses with another person make sure you make eye contact and let them know that you are acknowledging their existence and the toast.

龍牛

cultural communications

The following tips are generalities, followed by some tips that may be more country specific. People all over can be different to the expected norm for an area, but if you are aware of some of these differences and taboos it can save you from some very tricky situations.

Asia

- Handshakes are weaker than we are used to in Australia.
- Never assume a 'yes' means yes, it may mean 'I am listening'.
- When negotiating, start with plenty of options.
- Always present your business card face up and hand over with two hands, except in Hong Kong where a straight handover is customary.
- Never write on your business card or the receiving card in front of the person.
- Engraved business cards are considered prestigious.
- Always have your title on your card. Asians need to know if you are able to make decisions or not.

- Never place a received card straight into your pocket or card case. Leave it on the table you are at or hold it in your hand until you move away from the place you received it.
- Slightly bow to elderly people to show respect. This is acceptable in most countries, with the exception of China and Japan. In Japan they do not expect cultural niceties; they mean business.
- Accept all invitations. Social relationships will definitely help you.
- Karaoke is huge in Asia so get your voice ready for a good sing. You will be expected to sing and not just watch.
- Don't wear white to social functions as it represents death and mourning.
- Always start introductions with the most senior person.
- Aside from handshakes, pubic displays of affection are frowned upon by men and women but same-sex hand holding is acceptable.

- In public, do not walk or stand with your hands in your pocket.
- When using an interpreter, speak to the person you are in a meeting with and not the interpreter.
- When English is not the first language, speak clearly and avoid using jargon.
- When you need to refuse any favours, do so with a great deal of humility and be very apologetic.
- The guest of honour at a function will sit opposite the host, with the next most important people on the left and right of the guest.
- Expect to hear them burp and slurp as it is a sign they are enjoying their meal.

Indonesia

- Nothing will happen quickly.
- Indonesians value relationships and goodwill over business.

- If you are making a presentation in Indonesia have it translated onto Bahasa.
- Handshakes are softer and last for longer than a traditional Western shake.
- Public contact of a romantic nature is not acceptable to the Indonesians.
- Never touch the top of an Indonesian adult's head.
- Never show the bottom of your foot as it is considered unclean. Therefore do not sit with your foot across your knee.
- Pounding your fist into your palm can be perceived as indecent.
- While you will be on time, do not be surprised if your Indonesian guests aren't.
- Quiet tones of speech are more appreciated than excitable sounds and gestures.

Japan

- While a Japanese person will shake hands, you might wish to show your respect for the person by bowing.
- The thumb and forefinger sign (the 'okay' sign in Australia) means money to the Japanese.
- Blowing your nose is considered impolite. If you must, move away from the people you are with, use a tissue and dispose of it.
- To save face, politely side step any questions you don't wish to answer.
- Only make jokes that cannot cause offence to anyone.
- Save discussing any business for at least 15 minutes after meeting.
- The Japanese are very literal people and will not understand sayings like 'you're killing me' or 'you crack me up'.
- Group consensus prevails, so praise the group and not an individual.

- Often a pause in conversation is just a chance to mull over ideas, not a reason to butt in.

Malaysia

- Once you have signed a contract, the people you are doing business with may continue negotiations.
- Write acceptance letters to social events on red or pink stationery, never white.
- Business will not be discussed when spouses are present.
- Yellow is the colour of the sultans and traditionally avoided by many Malaysians.
- Remove shoes and sunglasses before entering a mosque.

China

- Bow or nod for an initial greeting and wait for the handshake.

- The Chinese are not overly emotive so do not expect too many smiles.
- Keep the situation formal and use surnames until invited to use first names.
- The first person to enter a room should be the most senior.
- The Chinese will expect to deal with the decision makers, yet they often leave theirs behind.
- If you are invited to a meeting you will be expected to leave first.
- Small talk is important at the beginning of all meetings. Ask about their family to show interest.
- Do not assume the Hong Kong locals are culturally the same as the Chinese.

The Philippines

- The raising and lowering of a person's eyebrows does not mean they are questioning you, but that they understand you.

- Raising your voice will have them thinking you are argumentative.
- Intermediaries are the best ones to initiate corporate/business negotiations for you.
- A Filipino may hand write their home number on a card so that you can call them at home on business matters. It does not necessarily mean they want to date you.
- Even when an established bond is made with a Filipino company, if you are new you will have to re-establish your own bond.
- Filipinos generally respond well to new ideas and concepts.
- Smiles can hide nervousness so a person may not be as happy as they seem.
- When invited to a Filipino home for dinner, arrive 15 to 20 minutes late.
- Never refer to someone's wife as the hostess. That title is used for prostitutes.

Singapore

- Competency and merit are highly valued by the Singaporeans.
- Tea drinking is a strong culture so business can be done as effectively over a cup of tea as a meal.
- Singaporeans are brought up under strict laws so don't drop litter, chew gum or jay walk there.

South Korea

- Bow at the beginning and the end of a meeting.
- Koreans are very emotional and outbursts are not uncommon, but it does not mean things are going badly.
- Heavy drinking is common and can go late into the evening, even on weeknights.
- Never start drinking until everyone has a full glass.
- South Koreans prefer to converse after a meal and concentrate on their food whilst eating.

- Forks should be used at all times. Never handle food with your fingers.

Taiwan

- To show great respect for a Taiwanese elderly person, cover your left fist with your right hand and raise both hands to your heart.
- Personal space is important so keep a distance of around two arm lengths.
- If you are not presented with a business card, the person has no desire to do business with you.
- Wait for an invitation to enter a room or sit in a chair before doing so.
- Handshakes may be replaced by a nod of the head by more traditional Taiwanese.
- Modesty is important: do not thank someone for a compliment and then insist you are not worthy at the same time. Take the time to compliment them.

Vietnam

- Whilst young Vietnamese are adopting Western attitudes, the general attitude is more reserved and not open to displays of affection.
- Referring to someone as a brother or nephew does not always mean a blood relation, but someone cared for and highly respected.
- Vietnamese men may still feel uncomfortable with Western women and expect them to sit with their women.
- Many Vietnamese in Australia have been here for decades and are more Western in their drinking habits.
- Business meetings may be held over dinner and proceed late into the evening.
- When whiskey or cognac is served during a meal it is customary to drink it after a toast.
- Gifts are commonly given and in many instances a token is considered more important for sentiment rather than price.

India

- The traditional greeting in India is the 'namaste'. Hold your palms together below your chin, bow and say 'Namaste'.
- To respond to a 'Namaste', after a handshake place your right hand over your heart.
- Whilst you may eat with your right hand, do not place it in a communal bowl on the table.
- Indians are very open and you can expect them to ask about your family in detail.
- Indians base arguments on feelings and faith as opposed to facts and data.
- Don't expect an argument if they believe their boss to be wrong.
- Indians are very caste (class) conscious. Caste is based on birth, occupation or social positioning.
- Ensure everything is put in writing so you can be sure that whatever you are discussing is understood.

- Decisions are made in accordance with the person's position in the family and social structure.
- When being entertained, it is customary to refuse the first offer and accept all future offers of beverages.
- Lunch is the preferred time to do business.
- If you receive a garland of flowers, remove them immediately to show humility.
- Many Indians are Hindu so be aware of their need to pray regularly.
- Do not greet an Indian with a hug or a kiss.
- Western women should not initiate shaking hands with an Indian man.

the Middle East

Israel

- Israelis are very forward and can ask many questions which may be deemed too personal by other cultures.
- Do not offer to shake hands with someone of the opposite sex until they offer first.
- Whilst hand gestures are fine, pointing is considered offensive.
- Men and women are considered equals.
- Business dealings need assurances for immediate rather than long-term gain due to a fatalistic style of thinking.
- Do not discuss families until you know the people personally.
- When dealing with an orthodox Jewish man, a woman should place items near him rather than hand them to him.

- In a business situation, an invitation will be made to the invitee first and then their spouse. Socially it will be the other way round.
- When travelling to Israel it is important for women to know and understand their dress codes. For men it is far more casual.

Saudi Arabia

- Men must cover everything from the navel to their knees, but don't consider wearing shorts there.
- Women must show respect by wearing modest dress; long sleeves and trousers or skirts are acceptable here.
- Whilst in Saudi Arabia transactions go at two speeds: either protracted or extremely fast. Do not be surprised if a delay can be finalised overnight.
- The preceding name *bin* means 'son of' and does not assume relation to any other person with *bin* in their name.

- Saudi princes should be referred to as 'His/Your Royal Highness'.
- In the West, most Saudis will wear suits, but at home they prefer local clothing consisting of outer robe, head scarf and rope.
- Saudi women may wear any style of clothing in private but must don an *abbaya* (black cloak) and head scarf in public.
- Any promotional material prepared for an Arabic country should include a local translation.
- Don't jump into disagreements; keep calm and speak in gentle tones.
- Avoid touching a Muslim child on the top of his or her head.

Europe/United Kingdom

Denmark

- Many Northern Europeans are honest communicators which can make them seem blunt at times. If a mistake is pointed out it is not to belittle you but to allow you to fix it.
- When in Northern Europe, use logic and facts in your presentations.
- Meetings move swiftly and are kept on time.
- The okay gesture of your finger and thumb joining can be an insult to a Dane.
- Men precede women up the stairs and women stay in front when descending.

- Passing people in a theatre-style presentation should be done facing the person to reach your seat.
- Denmark is a society based on equality, so both juniors and seniors are treated with equal respect.
- Denmark is a leader in business equality and many women hold high positions in this country.
- Stability is important to the Danes and if you can show longevity in business it will be appreciated.

Germany

- In a group, don't shake hands across someone else's handshake.
- Give praise for a job well done, but compliments can be viewed with suspicion.
- 'Hi, how are you?' will get a detailed answer as opposed to being considered a throwaway line.
- Germans out on business may not enjoy having every moment of the day filled. They like some time alone.

- Germans and other Northern Europeans can sound more forthright than they are due to the way their language translates.
- Show you know your material as they will be fully prepared.
- Do not discuss personal issues.
- Germans will often rap the table instead of clapping a presentation.
- Breakfast meetings are not part of their corporate culture.
- Dark shirts and red ties are rarely seen due to the uncomfortable reminder they give to past political regimes

Russia

- Keep eye contact during introductions for as long as you are addressed.
- Russians find it bad manners to sit on your coat at theatres and restaurants. Use the cloak room.

- Women are more likely to face challenges in business when dealing with Russian businesses.
- Do not serve any beverages in plastic cups in meetings.
- Always close the door behind you when leaving an office or meeting room.
- When invited out by Russian businessmen, do not expect your spouse to be invited.
- Don't start to eat until a toast has been made.
- Drinking alcohol is important in Russian culture so you will need to give a good excuse or be a good actor to save yourself from a honker of a hangover.
- Russian men will be insulted if women try to pay the bill at any dinners so accept their offer to pay or you will give offence.

Spain

- The Spanish are often heavy smokers so entertain them in smoker friendly places.
- Spanish men will give a short, firm handshake.

- Spanish women are more likely to kiss and hug you welcome.
- Spaniards have a very close personal space, so don't be surprised if they seem very touchy and close.
- Sexual stereotyping is easing, but many men still expect the woman to stay at home.
- Pride is everything to the Spanish so a woman may have difficulty dealing with a male ego.
- Dinner is often eaten well after 8 pm and goes late into the evening.
- Spaniards do not enjoy or relate well to sarcasm.
- In Southern Europe expect meetings to be flexible and not stick to the proposed agenda.
- The Southern Europeans are a very demonstrative people so you shouldn't assume they are angry until the mood escalates.

Britain

- The British tend to follow the establishment and rules. Make sure you understand how things are done in the area in which you work.
- A firm handshake is the accepted form of greeting.
- The British love humour and it can be quite slapstick at times.
- 'How do you do' is a greeting, and not to be confused with a question.
- The British tend to be less emotional and more in keeping with a stiff-upper-lip style of expression.
- While many British will use surnames only in reference to colleagues and friends, it is not to be done if you are not on close terms with a person.
- The British enjoy dressing for events so be aware of the dress code.
- In many clubs men are required to wear a shirt, tie and jacket.
- Business cards may not be presented till the close of a meeting.

North America

- North Americans will often leave their utensils crossed, even when they have finished eating.
- They have a habit of eating with their fork in their right hand.
- They are open to new ideas and well-presented ideas.

The United States

- Americans tend to make up their minds quickly and business moves quickly.
- Rather than sit in contemplative silence they will keep the conversation moving.
- Business styles are direct and a 'no' may come swiftly and definitely.
- Whilst the United States is the major world leader in many instances, it is ethnocentric and believes in its own superiority.

- Americans are not as globally aware as many other cultures.
- This is a very litigious society so dot your 'i's and cross your 't's.
- Drinking is not as common as in other cultures so do not be surprised if alcohol is not complementary at evening functions.
- Smoking is outlawed in many states in bars and restaurants. Be aware before you light up.
- Never assume a dark-skinned American is African American. They could be Creole and are usually proud of their ancestry.
- Dates are written month/day/year so 10 March 2005 will be 3/10/2005; not to be confused with October 3rd.

Canada

- Canadians should not be mistaken for Americans.
- Keep presentations and discussions simple and unexaggerated.
- Canadians resent people who push through queues.
- Parts of Canada are French speaking but most will be bilingual.
- No more than 15 minutes late is acceptable for a dinner invitation.
- Discussions will not be affected if you need to take over someone else's role.
- Humour is welcome in business.

South Africa

- Handshakes are firm and given to both men and women.
- The 'African handshake' (shaking and slipping your free hand around each other's thumb) never occurs between two Caucasian people.
- African men will generally precede a woman through the door.
- Whilst in South Africa never indicate the number two as a reverse facing peace sign or they will think you are giving them the finger.
- South Africans appreciate 'good breeding' and will respond well to a well-ranked education.
- The South African slang for a meal is 'graze'.
- Many deals are still sealed with a handshake so you can rest assured the deal is final at this stage.

New Zealand

- New Zealanders are used to being taken out socially when they start a new job and can be surprised at the lack of celebration and initiation when they start a new job in Australia.
- Do not treat them as a small country or a poor cousin.
- Prior to British colonisation, the Maori were the inhabitants of New Zealand. The traditional greeting among Maori is to rub noses but it is unlikely that you will encounter this in most corporate settings.
- Because of New Zealand's strong historical links with Britain, British customs and gestures are common. However, New Zealand is now a very culturally diverse country with strong influences from the Pacific Islands and Asia.
- To chew gum and use toothpicks in public is considered quite rude.

- New Zealand has two official languages: English and Maori. Both languages incorporate words from each other.
- A hangi is a traditional Maori feast of meats that are baked in the ground. Expect to be invited to enjoy seeing the meat being taken from the ground.

corporate golf

* **Get in the swing of things**

  Golf days are not just a day off work; they are potentially powerful networking days and should be attended where possible.

* **Know what you're doing to a tee**

  The rules for corporate golf days are slightly different to what you are used to when playing with your buddies on the weekend. They play an Ambrose style of competition.

* **Make use of your gifts**

  Before the game you could be handed some company branded balls or tees. Don't save them for later; use them during the day and enjoy them.

* **Be a good sport**

  So what if your game is off? Don't sit there and complain about the one that got away. Enjoy the day and the company and just maybe you'll be invited back next year.

✱ Understanding Ambrose: know your place

Playing in teams of four, you tee off in order of experience. The person with the least experience goes first and the one with the lowest handicap plays last. So if you are a good golfer you could have the company CEO playing before you on the tee. In this style of competition you play each shot from where the best shot lies. Therefore if you have gone into the bunker, the rough or the lake it doesn't matter. Grab your ball and head for the top spot. (Even the worst player can win.)

✱ Clothes maketh the man and the golfer

After the game you will be expected to meet in the club house for a drink. It is advisable to have a change of clothing. Forget your jeans. Whether it is a private or a public course, wear trousers in wool, cotton or moleskin and definitely a collared shirt. Your invitation will inform you if a jacket and tie are required for a dinner.

* Playing the part

If you are likely to be invited to a few golf days, buy yourself some golf shoes. Invitations to private courses will often insist on golf shoes being worn. Once again, forget your jeans and wear comfortable trousers and a collared shirt. If golf shoes are not requested and you don't own any, wear a flat soled shoe. A sand shoe or boat shoe is ideal. Leather and traction soled shoes will not be allowed on the course.

* Buggy etiquette

Yes, there is buggy etiquette. It is desirable to share the driving. Even if your clubs sit behind the passenger side of the cart, don't expect to be chauffeur driven around the course. Remember to drive to both balls. It is not acceptable to stop the buggy at the first ball and walk to the next. You go wherever the balls are.

*** Share the loss**

If someone hits their ball into the rough it is everybody's job to help find it. Do not leave the hunting up to the person who hit the ball while you all partake in some liquid refreshments from the buggy bar.

*** Who loses the ball?**

Only the loser of the ball can claim it is lost and stop the search. It is not anyone else's call.

*** Know your balls**

Before you start playing, let each other know which brand of ball you are playing with so no one can pretend a better shot is theirs.

*** From apprentice to captain**

This is a day when the best player leads. You may be only new to the company but if your golf game is good you can be the leader of the day.

* **The buggy bar**

  Don't drink too much alcohol during the day. Both your mind and your game can go off.

* **Team effort**

  Strategically, this can be the best way to form relationships with people from other businesses as you can have a whole day to get to know each other.

* **What you don't own can be hired**

  In many cases everything should be organised for you right down to your balls and tees but if it doesn't appear that way, you can often hire what you need from the course. Ask beforehand so you don't waste time when you arrive organising last minute hire.

Rules of the 19th hole

You can't leave your hat on. It is frowned upon and you can be asked to leave simply for wearing your hat/cap. When you are getting changed after the game, leave any hats or visors in your change bag.

Stick with the team. It is expected that the team that plays together stays together for at least one or two drinks. No matter how much you want to get with your buddies and compare scores, not sharing a drink with your team is a huge snub.

Loser shouts. Whoever had the worst round will shout the winners of the day their first round. This also gives you a chance to hob nob with the winning team.

Share the prize. It's a team win and it is expected that you share the prize evenly amongst the group.